P9-CPZ-858

Donna Jakob

My New Sandbox

Illustrated by
Julia Gorton

HYPERION BOOKS FOR CHILDREN
NEW YORK

There is a bug.
A black bug.
There is a black bug
waddling in the sand.

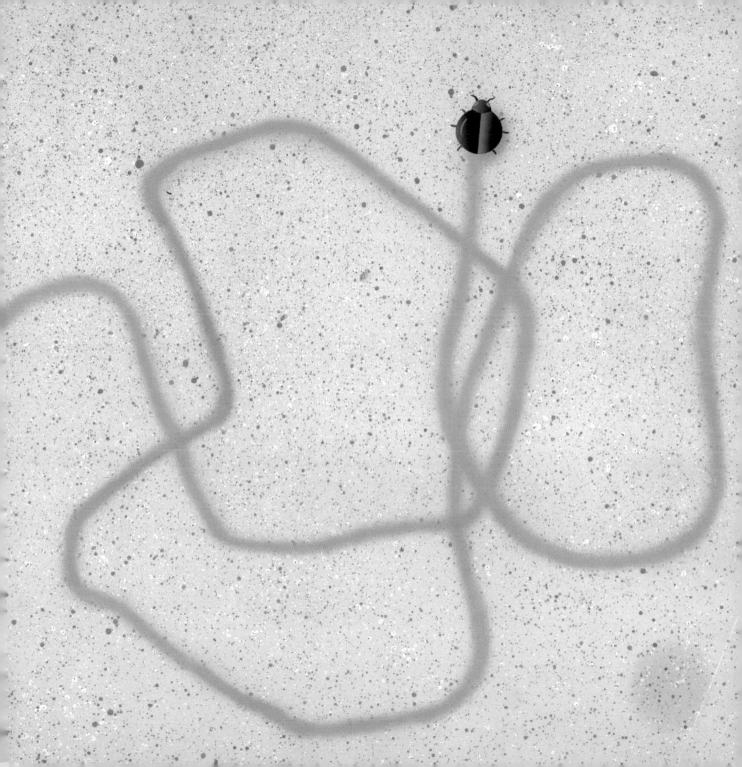

There is a **bird**.
A red bird.
There is a red bird
searching in the sand
in my new sandbox.

There is a **dog**.
A spotted dog
digging in the sand
in my new sandbox
that is in my backyard
and is just my size.

There are feet.
Two feet.
There are two feet
stomping in the sand
in my new sandbox
that is in my backyard
and is just my size.

Get out, bug.

Get out, bird.

Get out, dog.

Get out, feet.

get out of the sand
in my new sandbox
that is in my backyard
and is just my size.

Now I get in
my new sandbox.

I waddle in the sand.
I search and dig and
stomp in the sand.

But I am all alone
in the sand.
I am all alone
in my new sandbox
that is in my backyard
and is just my size.

Come back, black bug.
Come back and waddle
with me in the sand.

Come back, red bird.
Come back and search
with me in the sand.

Come back, spotted dog.
Come back and dig
with me in the sand.

Come back, two feet.
Come back and stomp
with me in the sand.

There is room for all of us

in the sand
in my new sandbox
that is in my backyard
and is just
our size.

For Jo, Charles, Howard, and James.
And for Mother and Daddy, who made room for all of us
—**D.J.**

To my mother and father, who helped me from sand to crayons to paint
—**J.G.**

For information address
Hyperion Books for Children,
114 Fifth Avenue,
New York, New York 10011-5690.
Printed in Singapore.

First Edition
1   3   5   7   9   10   8   6   4   2

Library of Congress Cataloging-in-Publication Data

Jakob, Donna
My new sandbox / Donna Jakob : illustrated by Julia Gorton—1st ed.   p.   m.
Summary: A child learns that his new sandbox is bigger than he
thought, big enough to share with some animal friends and playmates.
ISBN 0-7868-0172-7 (trade)—ISBN 0-7868-2144-2 (lib. bdg.)
[1. Sandboxes—Fiction. 2. Sharing—Fiction. 3. Play—Fiction.]
I. Gorton, Julia, ill. II. Title.
PZ7.J153554Myn 1996
[E]—dc20
95—21784

The artwork for each picture is prepared using airbrushed acrylic on paper.
This book is set in 24-point Oficina Sans Book.

Design and typography by Julia Gorton.